New Year

by

Michele Spirn

WORLD CELEBRATIONS AND CEREMONIES

BLACKBIRCH PRESS, INC.

WOODBRIDGE, CONNECTICUT

Published by Blackbirch Press, Inc.
260 Amity Road
Woodbridge, CT 06525

©1999 by Blackbirch Press, Inc.

First Edition

e-mail: staff@blackbirch.com

Web site: www.blackbirch.com

Printed in the United States

10 9 8 7 6 5 4 3 2 1

Photo Credits
Cover: Air-India Library; pages 3 and 22: ©Brent Peters; page 5: ©Mary Altier; pages 6 and 8: ©Jeffrey Aaronson/Network Aspen; page 7: ©John Dittli; page 9: ©Paul Thompson/International Stock; page 11: ©George F. Mobley/National Geographic Image Collection; page 13: ©Richard Lobell; page 15: ©Buddy Mays/Travel Stock; page 17: ©J. Highet/Trip Photographic Library; page 18: ©Suzanne Murphy-Larronde/DDB Stock Photography; page 20: ©The Image Bank; page 23: ©John G. Cardasis/International Stock.

**Library of Congress
Cataloging-in-Publication Data**
Spirn, Michele.
New Year / by Michele Spirn.
    p. cm. —(World celebrations and ceremonies)
    Includes bibliographical references and index.
    Summary: Describes how countries around the world traditionally celebrate the New Year, including rowdy parties, special feasts, and spiritual ceremonies and covering such countries as Brazil, China, and England.
    ISBN 1-56711-249-8 (lib. bdg. : alk. paper)
    1. New Year—Juvenile literature. [1. New Year. 2. Holidays.] I. Title. II. Series.
GT4905.S63 1999
394.261'4—dc21
                     98-12118
                     CIP
                     AC

☺ CONTENTS ☺

⑥ **INTRODUCTION** ⑥

All over the world people celebrate the New Year—the first day of the year. For some, the New Year starts on January 1, and celebrations begin the night before, on New Year's Eve. Others begin the New Year at a different time. Sometimes this is because their calendar is a lunar one. It is based on the movement of the moon around Earth. China and Israel keep lunar calendars. In the United States and in many other countries, people keep a solar calendar. It is based on the path of Earth around the sun.

Adults and children have many ways of welcoming the New Year. In Nigeria, children slam doors to frighten the old year away. Russian children go to parties to see Grandfather Frost and the Snow Maiden. Some people set off firecrackers. Others go fishing. In many places, families share a feast and eat foods that they hope will bring them good luck. All over the world people look forward to the New Year because it is a new beginning.

BRAZIL

In northern Brazil, a family gathers at someone's house for a New Year's Eve party on December 31. Outside, the streets are decorated with strips of brightly colored paper. Bells and flowers hang from street lamps. Inside, the table is set for a special meal of roast turkey, beef, or ham. After dinner, the family dances and sings. At midnight, church bells ring, car horns and sirens wail, and firecrackers pop. Inside, everyone hugs and shouts, "*Feliz Ano Novo*" (fay-LEES AHN-yo NO-vo). This means "Happy New Year" in Portuguese, the official language of Brazil.

After midnight, a late supper is served. In some parts of the country, it includes lentils because they are a symbol of wealth for the New Year. Other foods served might be codfish cakes and *rabanada* (rah-bah-NAH-dah), French toast topped with cinnamon and sugar. After supper, children go to bed, and grown-ups dress up and go to balls. They dance until the early morning. On New Year's Day, another meal is served. There are plenty of sweets, such as coconut pudding and marzipan— candies shaped like little fruits.

Key for All Country Maps
★ *Capital city*   ■ *Major city*

Brazilians like to dance in celebration of the New Year.

On the east coast of Brazil, those who worship in the Umbanda religion go to the beach on New Year's Eve. Some of them come from the city of São Paulo. They dress in white and bring fresh flowers, candles, and gifts

Brazil is the largest country in South America. Because Brazil is in the southern part of the world, the New Year occurs in the summer.

for the goddess Lemanja. At midnight, everyone runs into the water carrying flowers and gifts. If the waves carry the gifts out to sea, the goddess is happy, and they will have good luck in the coming year.

CHINA

In China, the New Year is also called
Spring Festival. It falls between January 21 and February 19, which is
early spring. The holiday is celebrated for 15 days. On New Year's
Eve, children help their families clean house and put up decorations.
During the two-week celebration, people do not clean their homes
because they believe they will sweep good luck out the door. Chinese
people think red is a lucky color. So they fill their homes with red
flowers and red scrolls—rolled up tubes of paper. The scrolls are like
New Year's cards. They wish everyone wealth and happiness.

On New Year's Eve, most families
have a feast and every family mem-
ber is invited. Oranges and apples
are on the table for good luck. Fish
is eaten because it is a symbol of
plenty. The feast often includes
dumplings, which are balls of
dough filled with pork. On the
last day of the celebration, sweet
dumplings filled with nuts and
sugar are eaten.

*Children in Beijing dress in costumes
for New Year's celebrations.*

The Lantern Festival takes place on the last day of the New Year celebration.

During the holiday, many firecrackers are set off to scare away any evil spirits. The New Year celebration ends with the Lantern Festival. People carry lanterns of all shapes and sizes. In the north, where it is cold, lanterns may be carved from ice. In southern cities, such as Guangzhou, lanterns are often made from silk.

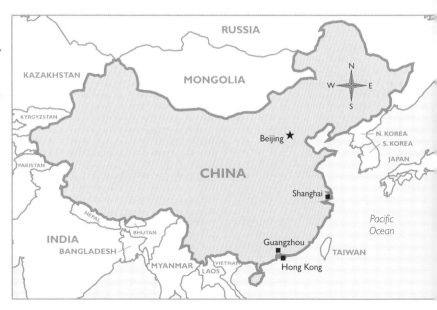

A "dancing dragon" is part of the Lantern Festival.

China has more people than any other country in the world. It has four times as many people as the United States. But the two countries are about the same size.

There is always a dancing dragon to bring people strength and good luck. The dragon is made from bamboo and is covered with colored paper or cloth. It is held up by as many as 50 men, who stand underneath it.

ENGLAND

On the night of December 31, many English people who live in London listen for the sounds of Big Ben, the city's largest clock. Some wait in outdoor squares, such as Picadilly Circus and Trafalgar Square. When they hear the clock's 12 loud gongs at midnight, they know it is the New Year. They shout and make noise and kiss each other.

English people think that the first person to come into the house on New Year's Day brings good or bad luck for the year. This person is called a "first footer."

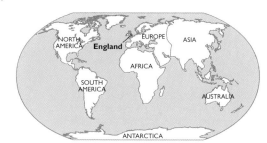

In some parts of England, a man with dark hair is supposed to bring good luck. In other parts of the country, blond or red hair are symbols of good fortune.

English children living near Scotland and Wales have lots of fun on New Year's Day. They go from house to house singing to their neighbors. The children wish them a happy New Year, filled with plenty of money and food. Then the children ask for a gift. They receive coins, apples, candy, or mince pies, which are filled with dried fruit. All singing has to stop by noon, when neighbors no longer give out presents. So it's not too surprising that children who live near Scotland and Wales get up early in the morning to get as many treats as they can!

In London, firecrackers explode over Big Ben.

England is part of the United Kingdom, which also includes Scotland, Wales, and Northern Ireland. The capital of the United Kingdom is London.

INDIA

In India, the New Year is called *Diwali* (dih-WAH-lee). It comes in the fall, when the Hindu people celebrate the return of the god Rama. According to the Hindu religion, Rama and his wife, Sita, were sent away by Rama's step-mother. Sita was

kidnapped by the evil ten-headed king Ravana. With help from a god, Rama fought and killed Ravana and rescued Sita. The people of India were so happy that Rama was coming home, they lit rows of candles. Today, oil lamps, electric lights, and candles are lit in homes and shops during *Diwali*. The word *diwali* means "light" in Hindi, the main language spoken in India. In small towns or in cities such as New Delhi, people paint and clean their homes, and children wear new clothes.

In some Hindu homes, prayers are said to Lakshmi, the goddess of wealth.

India is on the continent of Asia. This country is about one third the size of the United States. But it has more than three times as many people! The capital is New Delhi.

Indian children stand outside a hut that has been painted with decorations for Diwali.

Gifts of puffed rice, fruit, and silver coins are set before a statue of the goddess. A lighted clay pot filled with melted butter is also placed in front of her. Then family members sing songs to Lakshmi, thank-

ing her for bringing a new year and for giving them health and happiness. After praying and singing, adults and children enjoy a meal of vegetables. With it, they often eat a bread called *poori* (POO-ree) that is puffed up like a balloon. Children and adults then spend the evening watching fireworks.

Israel

In Israel, the Jewish New Year is called *Rosh Hashanah* (rosh ha-sha-NAH), which means "head of the year." This important holiday begins sometime in September or October. Jewish people believe that if you are sorry for anything bad you have done in the past year and pray to be forgiven, God will be understanding. The holiday begins in the evening, on *Erev* (EH-rev) *Rosh Hashanah*. Family members in the capital city of Jerusalem and all over Israel share a special meal. *Challah* (ha-LAH), a sweet egg bread, is baked into a round shape—the symbol of a full year and a long life. After a blessing is said over the bread, each person takes a piece and dips it in honey for a sweet New Year. A family might eat chicken soup with dumplings, roast chicken, noodle pudding, and honey cake.

The next day, everyone goes to synagogue, a house of prayer.

🌀 · 🌀 · 🌀 · 🌀 · 🌀 · 🌀 · 🌀 · 🌀 · 🌀 · 🌀 · 🌀

Israel is a very small country on the Mediterranean Sea. The capital is Jerusalem, which is 3,500 years old. It is a holy city for Jews, Christians, and Muslims.

🌀 · 🌀 · 🌀 · 🌀 · 🌀 · 🌀 · 🌀 · 🌀 · 🌀 · 🌀 · 🌀

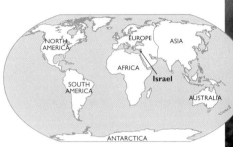

The cantor, who sings and leads the prayers, is dressed in white. The most exciting part of the service is the blowing of the *shofar* (sho-FAHR). It is a curved ram's horn that makes a trumpet-like sound. The *shofar* is blown several times to remind Jewish people to pray and ask forgiveness for their sins. At the end of the service, friends and relatives kiss and wish each other *L'Shana tova* (l'sha-NAH to-VAH), a "good year."

A shofar is blown during Rosh Hashanah.

MEXICO

In Mexico City and in other large cities, there are lots of things to do on New Year's Day. Families watch parades,

Mexico is south of the United States. The capital is Mexico City, one of the world's biggest cities. More than 20 million people live there.

go to horse races, and listen to guitar players. Many people have special dinners on this holiday, which Mexicans celebrate on January 1. A family might eat turkey covered with a special sauce called *mole* (MO-lay). It is sometimes made with bitter chocolate. Dessert might be *flan* (flahn), a pudding made from sugar, milk, and eggs.

In Mitla, in southern Mexico, the Zapotec people celebrate on New Year's Eve. They come to the city by bus, bike, or donkey. Some walk to Mitla carrying candles and torches. Adults build large fires. In the center of the light made by the candles and fires is a large cross. It is called the Cross of the Petition. Families place flowers near the cross and blow smoke from incense—a burning, perfumed stick—in four directions.

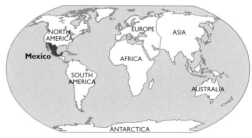

Flowers are an important part of the celebration called the Cross of the Petition.

Then they make small models of what they would like God to give them in the coming year. If a man wants a new house, he makes a tiny one out of sticks, with grass for a roof. If a family wants more pigs or sheep, a child might shape some animals out of seeds and plants. If someone wants to ask for large crops, she makes a row of straws. The Zapotec who cannot visit the cross bring their flowers and candles to special caves near their villages.

NIGERIA

All Nigerians think of January 1 as the start of the New Year. But people hold their celebrations at times that have special meaning for them. On December 31, Christians in cities such as Lagos dress in brightly colored clothes and go to church. The church bells ring at midnight, the beginning of

the New Year. People get down on their knees to ask God's blessing for the coming year. After prayers are over, people rise and greet each other with a New Year's wish.

The Igbo people celebrate the New Year in the spring. On March 18, everyone makes a lot of noise to show how sad the old year is to leave. Children run into their homes slamming their doors loudly. They believe if they're caught outside, the old year might take them with it. When the noise stops at midnight, families run outside to welcome the New Year by clapping.

Nigeria is in northwestern Africa, where it is always warm. In northern Nigeria, the weather is dry and hot. In the south, it is wet and steamy.

On New Year's Eve in Nigeria, Christians go to churches such as this one.

In northwestern Nigeria, the Kebbawa people celebrate February 10 as the New Year and the beginning of the fishing season. Thousands stand near the Sokoto River with nets. When a signal is given, they all jump into the river at the same time, and the frightened fish swim into the nets! Whoever catches the largest fish wins a prize.

PUERTO RICO

On December 31, families and friends gather together for big parties and New Year's Eve feasts. Favorite foods are roast pork and dumplings made out of potato and green-banana dough. For dessert, children love rice pudding with spices and coconut. At midnight, everyone eats 13 grapes. Twelve grapes are for sweet months in the coming year. The thirteenth grape is for good luck.

Atlantic Ocean

San Juan ★

Mayagüez

PUERTO RICO

Guayama

N
W ─✦─ E
S

Caribbean Sea

During the evening, the family might hear some singing outside. Every night from Christmas until January 7, groups of friends go from house to house playing music and singing. These people are called *parraderos* (pa-ra-DEH-ros). First, they sing outside a house.

On New Year's Eve in Puerto Rico, parraderos *go from house to house playing music and singing.*

Usually, they are invited in, and they are given food and drink. Afterward, they play music and everyone dances. Some *parraderos* make their own musical instruments. They make *maracas* (mah-RAH-cas) from

Puerto Rico is a small island southeast of Florida, in the Atlantic Ocean. It is always warm there, even on New Year's Day.

a vegetable called a "gourd." They hollow out the gourd, punch two small holes in it, and put in some pebbles. Then they put on a handle. When the *maracas* are shaken, they make a lot of noise. *Parraderos* also play drums and small guitars. Sometimes a family joins the *parraderos* and goes on to the next house. The group gets bigger and bigger as they go from house to house. Everyone has a good time dancing and singing until late at night.

RUSSIA

Russian children get their presents on New Year's Eve instead of on Christmas. Grandfather Frost brings the gifts. He is dressed like Santa Claus in a suit decorated

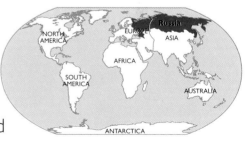

with fur. And he has a long white beard. But Grandfather Frost's suit is blue, and he does not come with reindeer. Instead, he travels with the Snow Maiden, who wears a fur-trimmed dress and tall boots.

Moscow is the capital of Russia. More than 50,000 decorated trees are placed all over the city for the New Year. Moscow gives Russia's best New Year's party for children. It is held in the Kremlin, the main government building. A clown standing at the door gives each child a present. A tall tree, full of shiny balls and colored lights, stands in the center of a large room. Everyone waits for Grandfather Frost, who arrives on a sled. Behind him come the Snow Maiden, snow bunnies, and children dressed in traditional Russian costumes. Boys wear baggy pants and boots. Girls wear fancy jumpers and blouses. The children in costumes sing. Dancers, magicians, clowns, and acrobats perform tricks, magic, and songs.

Russian folk dancers are part of Moscow's New Year's festival.

Then special food is served. Children may eat a soup made from beets, called *borsht*. Meat-filled dumplings and sweet cakes are other treats. The party-goers return home in good spirits, ready to begin the New Year.

Russia is a very large country. It covers the eastern part of Europe and stretches across northern Asia. Most of the year, more than half of the country is covered with snow.

UNITED STATES

In the United States, many people love to celebrate New Year's Eve. At midnight in New York City, thousands go to Times Square and wait for a large ball of light to drop from the top of a skyscraper. In Boston, the celebrations held around the city are called First Night.

Men and women ride in a colorful float in California's Tournament of Roses Parade.

Families and friends go from place to place to hear music, see puppet shows, and to dance. In Washington, D.C., and in many cities and towns, New Year's Eve is a time for parties. People wear funny hats, blow noisemakers, and throw confetti—pieces of colored paper.

On New Year's Day, some adults and children make resolutions. A New Year's resolution is a promise to yourself to improve something in the New Year. For example, a child may decide to study harder.

Many cities and towns have special celebrations on New Year's Day. In Pasadena, California, there is the Tournament of Roses Parade. It has been held every year for over 100 years! All the floats are decorated entirely with flowers. A woman is chosen to be the Rose Queen. After the parade, there is a big football game. In Philadelphia,

The United States is one of the largest countries in the world. It has a great mix of cultures. This means New Year's is celebrated differently around the country.

the Mummers' Parade lasts for ten hours. King Momus—a man dressed in a fancy costume—leads the parade. Clowns, dancers, and musicians all take part. More than 1 million people stand outside to watch the Mummers' Parade, even in cold or wet weather.

The Mummer's Parade in Philadelphia is a New Year's tradition.

Glossary

float A moving platform that is decorated for a parade.

confetti Pieces of colored paper thrown at a parade.

lunar calendar A calendar based on the movement of the moon around Earth.

maracas A pair of musical instruments made from hollowed-out gourds.

resolution A promise to improve something in the future.

symbol An object that represents something else.

Further Reading

Bernhard, Emery. *Happy New Year!* New York: Lodestar Books, 1996.

Chambers, Catherine. *Chinese New Year* (World of Holidays series). Chatham, NJ: Raintree/Steck-Vaughn, 1997.

Deshpande, Chris. *Diwali* (Celebrations series). New York: A&C Black, 1995.

Halliburton, Warren J. *Celebrations of African Heritage* (Africa Today series). Glendale, CA: Crestwood House, 1992.

Kimmel, Eric A. *Days of Awe: Stories for Rosh Hashanah and Yom Kippur.* New York: Viking Press, 1991.

Silverthorne, Elizabeth. *Fiesta!: Mexico's Great Celebrations.* Brookfield, CT: Millbrook Press, 1992.

Tourism Web Sites

Brazil: http://www.brazilinfo.com
China: http://www.Chinatourpage.com
England: http://www.visitbritain.com
India: http://www.tourindia.com
Israel: http://www.goisrael.com
Mexico: http://www.mexico-travel.com

Nigeria:
http://sas.upenn.edu/African_Studies/Country_Specific/Nigeria.htm

Puerto Rico:
http://www.Welcome.toPuertoRico.org

Russia: http://www.tours.ru

United States: http://www.united-states.com

Index